DISNEY PRINCESS

Palace Pets

Treasure

Ariel's Curious Kitten

By Tennant Redbank

Illustrated by Francesco Legramandi
and Gabriella Matta

Random House 🏠 New York

Treasure leaped onto the wooden table in the middle of the room. Princess Ariel was perched there next to a map of the world. Treasure nosed Ariel's hand aside for a better view.

Prince Eric pointed to a spot at the far edge of the paper. "Right there, Ariel," he said. "That's where I'm headed. Across the ocean, past the maelstrom, to the other side of the world!"

Treasure's nose twitched. Ocean? Maelstrom? Other side of the world? It sounded like an adventure. And Treasure loved adventures!

That was how the kitten had met

Princess Ariel—on a great adventure! Treasure had stowed away on Eric's ship. Princess Ariel came on board and spotted her. Right away, they became good friends.

Ariel leaned forward to study the map. "Ooh," she said. "I can't wait! When do we leave?" She looked up at Eric with wide eyes.

Treasure watched Eric, too. She hoped he would say soon. Like tomorrow—or even today!

Eric backed away from the table. "*We?*"

he said. "Ariel, this could be a dangerous trip. There will probably be, uh . . . sea monsters! And, um, terrible storms. Did I mention the maelstrom?"

Ariel shook her head. "I can handle it," she said. "Remember, I outswam sharks. I fought a sea witch. I saved YOU from drowning!"

Eric put his hands on her shoulders. "Believe me, I know," he said. "But you're needed *here*. Someone has to watch over the kingdom." He rolled up the map. "Besides, I'll only be gone a few months."

Ariel's mouth dropped open. Treasure's tail swished dangerously.

"A few *months*?" Ariel said. "That's forever! I'm coming with you."

"Your father would have my head if anything happened to you," Eric said. "I need to know you're safe." He kissed the top of Ariel's head, then took the map and left the room.

Treasure meowed. Poor Ariel! If Eric had told Treasure she couldn't go on the trip, she would have been crushed. And Ariel loved adventures as much as her kitten did. It wasn't fair that she couldn't go!

Treasure climbed into Ariel's lap and licked her hand. She would miss Ariel. She'd have to find a special gift to bring

back for the princess. Maybe a pretty shell . . .

"Treasure, I know the ocean inside and out. After all, I lived there most of my life," Ariel said, stroking Treasure's fur. "I'm going on that ship!"

Yes! Treasure knew one thing for sure: Ariel usually made things happen. If she wanted to go on this trip, she would go on this trip.

And Treasure would do everything she could to help!

Eric's ship was anchored at the dock in front of the castle. Treasure strolled up the gangplank. Right away, she felt at home.

The deck rocked gently beneath her paws. She looked around. The wood shone. The brass gleamed.

"Ahoy, Treasure!" Max, Eric's shaggy sheepdog, hailed her. He bounded over and gave her cheek a sloppy lick.

Treasure laughed. "Ahoy, Max!" She wiped the drool away with her paw. "Ahoy, Seashell!" she greeted the purple pony next to him.

Seashell had been born a sea horse. But she wanted to live on land so badly that Ariel had asked King Triton to make her a real horse. Now she lived at the castle, too. But she spent a lot of time on the water.

Max sat on his back legs. A sea breeze ruffled his fur and Seashell's mane.

"I can't wait until the ship casts off tomorrow," Max said.

Tomorrow? Treasure purred. Oh, good! They'd be leaving soon!

"I can't wait, either," Treasure said. She took a deep breath. She loved the smell of the salty air.

"You're coming?" Max asked.

"Of course!" Treasure said. How could Max think she'd stay behind? Now she just had to figure out how to convince Prince Eric to let Ariel go, too!

Treasure moved aside as a sailor bustled by. "We have a lot to do," she pointed out. "All hands—and paws—on deck!"

"And hooves!" Seashell added. "Don't forget about hooves!"

Treasure, Max, and Seashell helped the sailors stock the ship. Max rolled barrels of water across the deck. Seashell hauled

coils of rope around her neck. Treasure

dragged sacks of medicine on board. Each

sailor loaded a sea trunk. Their trunks

usually held clothes, shoes, and a book.

Treasure nudged a sewing kit into a

corner of the deck. She loved that about

a ship—everything had a special spot.

Then she stopped to look around. Eric was talking with his servant, Grimsby, by the ship's wheel. Maybe now was a good time to help Ariel!

"Let's report for duty," Treasure called to Max and Seashell.

Max bounded over to Eric. "Hey, boy!" Eric said. He knelt next to Max and ran his hand through the dog's thick fur. "Ready for an adventure?"

Max barked loudly.

Treasure leaped to the ship's wheel and meowed. Yes! She was ready, too!

Eric patted her head. "Oho!" he said. "You want to come?"

Treasure purred and rubbed her back against Eric's wrist. Her eyes closed.

"I should have guessed," he said. "But I need you to stay here with Ariel."

Treasure's eyes popped open.

What? Stay here? Was Eric crazy? There was adventure on the ocean, and she wanted to be a part of it!

Eric looked over the deck rail at the castle and frowned. "Ariel's not too happy about my leaving her behind," he said.

"Are you sure it's a good idea?" Grimsby asked. "If I may say, Princess Ariel is a wonderful sailor. Perhaps she should come."

Eric ran a hand through his hair. "It's too dangerous, Grim. I couldn't stand it if anything happened to her! No. It's you and me and Max on this trip."

"I could stay—" Grimsby began.

But Eric had already turned to pick up Treasure. He carried her down the gangplank and set her on the beach. "Take good care of my princess," he said.

Then he went back to the boat.

Treasure narrowed her eyes. Now she knew exactly how Ariel felt. It was no fun being left out! Sure, someone had to look after the kingdom. But there were plenty of people who could do that. It didn't have to be Ariel and Treasure.

Come heck or high water, Treasure was going to be on that ship!

Treasure sat on the beach and stared at the ocean. How could she get a message across to Eric? It was so hard. Humans never understood her purrs and meows.

If only she could write a note! But she had never learned her letters.

Treasure raked her claws across the sand. They made four deep lines. The lines almost looked like waves. . . .

That was it! Treasure would leave a message for Eric . . . in the sand!

All she needed was something to draw with. She ran up the beach to the dunes. There had to be something. . . .

Aha!

Treasure dug a skinny piece of driftwood out of the sand. It was perfect.

But when Treasure tried to draw, the lines came out all funny. *Hmph!* This wasn't as easy as she'd thought!

When she tried again, she heard a *clickety-clack* noise. She smiled. That sound could mean only one thing: Sebastian!

Sebastian the crab was Ariel's good friend. He clicked his way up the beach to Treasure. Behind him, a fish popped his head above the surf. That was Flounder, Ariel's best friend under the sea. And with a flurry of feathers, Scuttle the seagull landed on the sand beside his new friends.

"Wow, Treasure, whatcha doing?" Flounder asked.

"Trying to draw a ship," Treasure said. She lowered her voice to a whisper. "I want to convince Eric to take me and Ariel on his trip!" She told Sebastian, Flounder, and Scuttle all about it. And about how Eric didn't want Ariel or Treasure to go.

"That thingamajingy is a ship?" Scuttle asked. He pointed a wing at the drawing. "Looks more like a doodlehickey to me."

"Allow me," Sebastian said with a bow.

Treasure passed the stick to Sebastian. First she had him draw the ship. He made it huge. It took up nearly the whole beach, from the dunes to the surf. There was no way Eric would miss it.

He added waves at the bottom of the ship. Then he drew sails on the mast.

"Now draw Eric by the ship's wheel!" Treasure directed. "And Max, of course."

After he did that, he put Ariel at the front of the ship. Next to her, he drew a kitten. That was Treasure!

Treasure stepped back to admire

Sebastian's sand picture. It looked great!

At her side, Sebastian nodded. "That drawing is as clear as creek water," he said. "I only worry 'bout one thing."

"What?" Treasure asked.

"I worry 'bout—"

"Caw! Caw!" Scuttle cut off Sebastian's answer. He circled his friends over the beach. "Eric's leaving the ship! He's coming this way!"

Treasure snapped to attention. Eric was headed toward her! He would see the drawing. He would know he had to take

them on the trip! She couldn't wait!

She positioned herself next to the drawing. She held her head high and faced Eric.

Out in the water, Treasure heard Flounder cry, *"Whee!"*

What is he doing? Treasure thought. She turned to see him riding a big wave toward the shore. She smiled. Then her smile became a frown.

A big wave? Oh, no!

With a sound like thunder, the wave crashed onto the sand.

The surf roared up the beach.

Treasure ran in front of the water. But she couldn't stop it. It rolled right over Sebastian's drawing.

When the wave rolled back, her ship was wiped away. The drawing of Ariel,

Eric, Max, Seashell, Treasure, and the ship—gone. Only the top of the mast was left.

Eric walked past. "Hi there, Treasure!" he called. "Hey, Sebastian, Flounder, Scuttle! Enjoying this fine day?"

Treasure's ears drooped.

Sebastian lowered his head sadly. "High tide," he said. "Dat is what I was worried 'bout."

4

Treasure shook sand from her fur. She moped past the dunes. She moped past the landing. She moped up to the seawall. She found Ariel sitting there, cross-legged. The princess was staring at the sea.

Treasure leaped up next to her.

"Oh, hi, Treasure," Ariel said. "I've been trying to think of ways to convince Eric to take me on the trip."

Treasure meowed. Her too!

"So far I've got nothing," Ariel added. "We've spent so much time together on the water. On his ship . . . in rowboats . . . I can't believe he doesn't want me to go!"

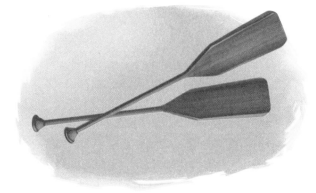

Treasure's ears pricked up. Wait a second. Maybe if Eric saw Ariel—and Treasure—on a boat, he would remember what good sailors they both were!

Treasure jumped to her paws. She took Ariel's skirt in her teeth and tugged.

"Sorry, I don't have time to play," Ariel said. "I need to— Oh, are you trying to show me something?"

Treasure pulled Ariel to the landing. A small rowboat was tied there.

"You want to go rowing?" Ariel said. She stepped toward the boat. Then she stopped and grinned at Treasure. "Hey, we should get Eric to come, too! He'll remember all our other boat trips. He won't want to leave me behind!"

Ariel dashed off, calling over her shoulder. "Wait here! I'll be right back . . . with Eric!"

Treasure curled up on the dock. Her plan was working!

Then she heard hoofbeats on the wooden dock.

"Hey, Treasure," Seashell said. "Taking a nap?"

"No!" Treasure said. She was not the kind of kitten who took naps. "I'm waiting for Ariel and Eric to get back. We're going for a boat ride."

"Can I come?" Seashell asked.

"I don't know," Treasure said. She eyed the rowboat. "It's not a very big boat."

"I'm not a very big pony," Seashell pointed out.

The sound of laughter kept Treasure from answering. Ariel and Eric were walking along the dock. Actually, Ariel was pulling Eric along the dock.

"Come on," she told him. "It will be fun. We won't get to see each other for months and months and months."

Eric looked sad at the thought. "Okay," he said. "But I've got a lot to do. I still have to pack my trunks. Two of them!"

He held out a hand to help Ariel into the boat, but she jumped in on her own. Treasure leaped too.

"Okay, you can come," Eric said to Treasure. He sat down and took the oars.

Ariel untied the rope that held the boat to the dock. She pushed them off. The boat floated away from the shore. As it did, Seashell whinnied. She reared back, ready to jump.

Treasure hissed a warning. If Seashell jumped, the boat would capsize for sure!

Too late. Seashell tucked her heels under her and leaped across the gap. She landed in the boat—off center. The boat rocked hard. Ariel, Eric, and Treasure tried to balance it out. Then . . . the boat tipped over!

Splash!

Ariel, Eric, Treasure, and Seashell were dumped into the water.

Luckily, they all were strong swimmers. Ariel and Seashell had grown up in the sea. Treasure loved water more than land. They swam to the dock and, one by one, pulled themselves up.

While Eric dumped the seawater out of his boots, Ariel turned to Treasure. "Well, Treasure," she whispered, "that didn't go the way I planned!"

Treasure hardly slept all night. Eric's ship was leaving early in the morning. And she was out of ideas. She couldn't think of any way to convince Eric to take them along.

Treasure watched the sunrise from the window ledge. Her eyes were drawn to the dock. She wanted to be on that ship!

Behind her, Treasure heard a door

close softly. Then she saw Ariel tiptoe past her perch.

Where was the princess going?

Treasure knew one way to find out—follow her!

Ariel sneaked down the castle hallway. She opened a wooden door and slipped inside. Two trunks sat in the middle of

the room with their lids open. They were filled with clothes and maps and books. Carved into the side of each trunk was a large *E*.

Ariel hurried over to the larger trunk. She lifted out a heavy wool cloak and three linen shirts. She swung her leg over the side of the trunk, and then . . . Ariel climbed inside! She pulled the clothing she had taken out on top of her.

Treasure arched her back. Oh, Ariel was so smart! She was stowing away in Eric's trunk! Eric's sailors would load

the trunks onto the ship. Now they'd be loading Ariel, too!

Treasure wasn't about to be left behind. Besides, she knew a thing or two about stowing away. She leaped to the lid of the smaller trunk, balancing on the edge for a moment. Then she jumped inside.

Treasure dug under the piles of clothes. She found a nice soft spot next to Eric's pillow. She wiggled under a pair of breeches and curled up to wait.

Before long, Treasure heard the sound of boots clomping on the castle floor.

Someone shut the lid of the trunk. She felt the trunk being lifted. It tilted downward when it was carried down the stairs. She heard waves crashing on the shore. They must have been crossing the beach. The trunk tilted upward as they climbed the gangplank. Then the trunk was set down. The footsteps faded away.

Treasure waited. She heard pipe whistles. She heard sailors calling. The ship swayed back and forth. The scent of salt air got stronger. They were out to sea!

Treasure shook off the breeches. She

dug herself out of the layers of clothes. With both paws, she pushed open the trunk's lid. She looked out—

Right at Ariel's shocked face!

"Oh!" Ariel said, bursting into laughter. "I guess we had the same idea!"

She lifted Treasure out of the trunk. "I'll tell you a secret, Treasure. I couldn't stand to stay at the castle," she said. "And Grimsby couldn't stand to get on the ship. So we switched! He stayed behind to watch over things. I said goodbye to Eric and then snuck in here. You know Eric won't notice until later. He's always so busy when we set sail."

Treasure meowed. That made sense. She'd seen Grimsby turn green on sea voyages before. He liked land much better!

Ariel bit her lip. "Now I just have to tell Eric," she said.

Treasure followed Ariel to the deck. Sailors rushed back and forth. They pulled on ropes and fastened down lines.

Treasure looked up at the mast. A strong wind was blowing from the north.

The flag stood out stiffly from the pole. Dark clouds raced across the sky. Fat raindrops left large spots of water on the deck.

"Uh-oh," Ariel said. "Looks like we've sailed into a storm!"

The ship climbed a large wave and plunged down it. Water splashed over the side of the ship. Ariel grabbed the railing. Treasure braced herself against the deck.

Suddenly—*fwap, fwap, fwap, fwap*. Treasure heard a sound no sailor wants to hear on a ship. One of the sails was flapping free! Eric couldn't steer the boat without the sail to catch the wind.

"Get that sail secured!" Eric yelled over the wind and rain.

"Aye, aye!" two sailors called back. They scrambled up the mast. They reached for the sail, but they couldn't grab it without going out on the crossbar. They were too big, though. It was too risky in such a storm.

"Someone fix that sail!" Eric yelled.

But who? Eric and all the sailors were too heavy to climb out on the delicate crossbar. The only one on the ship small enough was . . .

Treasure!

Right away, Treasure launched herself at the mast. It was slick with rain. Her claws slipped. Then she caught herself.

Max barked from the front of the ship. "Go, Treasure!" he called. "You can do it!"

Eric needed her help. She had to try her best!

Treasure dug in her claws and climbed the mast. She passed the first sailor. She passed the second sailor. Treasure picked her way along the slippery crossbar.

Fwap, fwap, fwap. The sail whipped in the wind and rain.

Treasure stretched forward. She grabbed the rope of the flapping sail. Now how could she tie it down?

"I got it!" Ariel's voice said behind her. Treasure glanced over her shoulder. Ariel had followed Treasure to help with the sail!

Treasure held the sail tight. Ariel tied it into place.

Right away, the ship turned with the

wind. Eric had control again! Instead of getting pushed sideways by the waves, the ship was able to cut through them.

Treasure and Ariel shinnied down the mast. Max was waiting for them on the deck. Treasure jumped onto his shoulder and shook the rain from her fur.

As Ariel's feet touched the deck, Eric took her hand. His face looked as stormy as the sky. "Ariel," he said. "Treasure."

Treasure ducked her head. Eric hadn't wanted them to come. He must be furious!

But then his face broke into a huge

grin. "That was an amazing feat of seamanship! I don't think the ship could have stood many more of those big waves."

"You're not mad?" Ariel asked. "It was hardly safe."

"Mad?" Eric said. He put one arm around Ariel's shoulder. With the other, he lifted Treasure up. "When I spotted this kitten bravely climbing that mast— and then you, right behind her—I never felt so grateful to see anyone in my life!"

Ariel leaned in and stroked Treasure's back. "I was just following Treasure's lead," she said. She was so proud!

The rain beat down on Treasure's fur. A chilly wind whistled past her ears. The ship rolled with the storm. Thunder crackled in the distance.

Warmth? Dry fur? Solid land? Let other kittens have them. Treasure preferred a ship. And the ocean. And an adventure!

Eric shook his head. "Next time, I'll know better," he said. "I should never go sailing without you two treasures!"

Each Palace Pet has a story

Cinderella

Bibbidy

Snow White

Berry

Aurora

Beauty